DREAMWORKS

HOW TO TRAIN YOUR

DRAGON

THE HIDDEN WORLD

JOURNEY TO NEW BERK

ADAPTED BY **DELPHINE FINNEGAN**

ILLUSTRATED BY **PATRICK SPAZIANTE**

Simon Spotlight

New York London Toronto Sydney New Delhi

SIMON SPOTLIGHT
An imprint of Simon & Schuster Children's Publishing Division
1230 Avenue of the Americas, New York, New York 10020
This Simon Spotlight paperback edition January 2019
How to Train Your Dragon: The Hidden World © 2019 DreamWorks Animation LLC. All Rights Reserved.
All rights reserved, including the right of reproduction in whole or in part in any form.
SIMON SPOTLIGHT and colophon are registered trademarks of Simon & Schuster, Inc.
For information about special discounts for bulk purchases, please contact Simon & Schuster Special Sales
at 1-866-506-1949 or business@simonandschuster.com.
Manufactured in the United States of America 1218 LAK
2 4 6 8 10 9 7 5 3 1
ISBN 978-1-5344-3840-8
ISBN 978-1-5344-3841-5 (eBook)

Life on the island of Berk was very, very busy. Dragons filled the air. They took off and landed all day and night. Every house had a tower custom made for a dragon. More dragon houses were scattered across the island like barnacles. Even the village streets were crowded with dragons . . . and Vikings, too.

For the past year Hiccup and the Vikings he led had become dragon rescuers. They were dedicated to saving dragons who'd been captured by ruthless hunters. Once freed, the dragons were led to Berk to live in peace and to come and go as they pleased. It was exactly how Hiccup had imagined life on Berk—Vikings and dragons living peacefully together.

Not everyone was thrilled with this arrangement. Some dragons kept getting caught over and over again.

"You brought back a Hobgobbler? We're cursed," said Gobber. Everyone knew that Hobgobblers were bad omens.

"Gobber, relax. We did it. The world's first 'dragon-Viking utopia.' We made the dream a reality," replied Hiccup.

Gobber knew what Toothless, Hiccup's beloved dragon, meant to Hiccup and how content his former apprentice was running Berk as a haven for dragons. Still, he wanted more for the new chief of Berk.

"It's time to stop worrying about the problems out there and start sorting out the ones right here. Hang up those saddles and get married. . . . Start ruling like a proper royal couple." Then he whispered, "Marry him, please," to Hiccup's girlfriend, Astrid.

Out there, though, the problems were only getting worse. Warlords, who paid hunters to capture dragons, wanted Toothless, the Alpha of all dragons. If they could seize him, all other dragons would follow.

Inside a massive arena, soldiers trained armored dragons to fight one another. Dragons who weren't being trained were forced into cramped cages. Small doses of venom were used to sedate them.

The warlords had invited Grimmel, the most ruthless dragon hunter, to the arena. They needed his help and were willing to pay him a lot.

The warlords were tired of their hunters being attacked by Hiccup and his band of Dragon Riders. This didn't interest Grimmel until he heard that a Night Fury led the raids.

Back on Berk, Toothless had just finished gliding lessons with Hiccup. He still couldn't fly without Hiccup's help. As he walked through the forest, he heard groaning. He followed the sound and found something extraordinary. It was a Light Fury—a sleek, smooth white dragon. She had long, folded wings, similar to Toothless's. Her scales shimmered.

They were able to communicate without speaking. The Light Fury warned Toothless with a low growl: *It's a trap*. As they stared at each other in wonder, Hiccup and Astrid found them. The Light Fury did not like humans, so she flew away and then seemingly vanished into thin air.

After some investigating with Toothless, Hiccup realized that the Light Fury had been placed in the woods as bait. Hiccup talked with his friends about his discovery. Eret knew instantly who'd set the trap. Where Eret was from, Grimmel was famous for capturing Night Furies like Toothless.

That night, Grimmel boldly paid a visit to Hiccup's house. He tried to scare Hiccup into giving Toothless to him, but Hiccup steadfastly refused.

Grimmel told him, "You are going to give me that dragon. . . . Have my dragon ready when I return . . . or I will destroy everything you love."

The next morning, Hiccup knew he had to act. If he wanted to save the dragons' lives and protect their freedom, then he had to do something bold. He remembered a story his father had told him. It was an old sailor's tale of a land beyond the edge of the world. They called it the Hidden World—a land of dragons where no one could reach them. Hiccup's mom, Valka, remembered the story too.

"The few sailors who returned saw dragons guarding the entrance. There are great waterfalls leading to a land beneath the sea," Stoick had told him.

Hiccup was determined to find that place. Everyone on the island of Berk, including the dragons and especially Toothless, had to disappear!

The entire population of Berk followed Valka's lead and packed up and left their homes. They gathered everything they could and then added a little more. One Viking ship was filled to the brim with supplies, the other with sheep. The dragons helped.

"Is there an actual plan?" Gobber asked Hiccup.

"Just keep flying until we reach the end of the world," Hiccup answered.

Not long after they left, Toothless heard something. It was the Light Fury. She was following them! She blasted a fireball, disappeared for a moment, and then reappeared. Then she attacked Hiccup. As he fell to the water she expressed to Toothless, *You're free!* Instead of following her, Toothless chose to rescue Hiccup. The Light Fury couldn't understand why Toothless would stay with humans, so she flew away.

When Toothless pulled Hiccup out of the water, the Vikings laughed until they saw what was ahead of them. Suddenly, a towering island appeared. Cliffs as far as the eye could see broke through a ring of clouds surrounding the island.

The island was beautiful. It had everything they could want—lakes, forests, waterfalls, and so much land.

"Welcome to New Berk," proclaimed a Viking named Hoark.

Everyone started to talk about what they could build and do on this new island. Everyone except Hiccup. He was still thinking about the Hidden World.

"Hold on, gang. I said make camp, not build a new village," announced Hiccup.

Like Hiccup, Toothless did not want to stay on the island. He needed to find the Light Fury. He didn't have to worry, though—that night she found him at Hiccup's tent! Toothless followed her to a lake nearby. Toothless tried to dance with the graceful Light Fury, but he wasn't any good. Hiccup watched from above as his friend struggled.

Then Toothless drew a picture of the Light Fury. That seemed to impress her. They nuzzled noses and drew closer. But when the Light Fury wanted to fly away with Toothless, he could not follow her. Once again, his broken tail fin kept him from flying on his own.

Hiccup had a plan. He made a new tail fin for Toothless with gears that could move and mirror the actions of the adjacent tail fin. He covered it in a mortar made from ground-up scales that Toothless had shed. And it was fireproof. With a little bit of practice, Toothless would fly on his own!

Toothless was so excited. That night he met the Light Fury. They practiced shooting fireballs, and she taught him how to disappear, then reappear. As they flew through the moonlit sky she brought him to a hole in the sea surrounded by waterfalls. It was also her home. Together, they plunged down into the vast hole.

Back at the camp, Toothless was nowhere to be found, and Hiccup was worried. He knew Grimmel wouldn't stop until he captured Toothless. And they still hadn't found the Hidden World. While everyone else celebrated their new home, Hiccup hatched another plan. What if he turned the tables on Grimmel and captured him? Surely that would keep Toothless and the other dragons safe. Would his plan work? Only time would tell.